The Boy Who Became A Bear

By Jean McLaughlin

Illustrations By Natalie de Stefano

To order additional copies of this book, contact:
Xlibris Corporation
1-888-795-4274
www.Xlibris.com
Orders@Xlibris.com

Chapter I

Many years ago in a far off land lived a curious boy named Stefan. He had laughing brown eyes and golden blond hair and a deep yearning in his heart for adventure. No one in his rather large family suspected his secret. His three younger brothers and three younger sisters seemed quite content with life on their farm. His parents had never dreamed of traveling beyond the fertile valley surrounding their home. Only Stefan seemed to wonder what lay beyond the familiar fields and orchards.

Stefan's family had lived for generations in a large, sturdy old wooden farmhouse. The farm, with its rich plowed fields, lay in a beautiful valley below a dark and mysterious mountain forest. Stefan often paused to gaze at the forest while he milked the brown goat or chopped more firewood, wondering what secrets lay hidden within the deep green shadows of the trees.

Stefan loved his family very much and he loved their farm, but every day seemed very much like the next. Everyone rose before dawn to do the endless chores. Stefan fetched water, lit fires and fed the pigs, cows, horses and goats. In the spring he plowed the fields, in summer he tended the crops, and in the fall he helped with the harvest. At the end of the day, the family gathered for dinner together in the vast kitchen around the wooden table. Soon after sunset, Stefan went to bed in the small room he shared with his three little brothers.

Natali de Stefano '99

Stefan had only one event to look forward to with excitement. Every Saturday in the summer and autumn the family rose before dawn and carefully loaded their large wagon with fresh vegetables, milk and eggs to take into the village. Stefan and his brothers harnessed Sam, their huge brown draft horse, to the wagon and the whole family piled in for Market Day.

Stefan always enjoyed Market Day. Everyone he knew would be bustling around the village square, buying, selling, or just having fun. After he helped his parents set up their own stall, he was free to go have fun, too. Stefan saw his friend Mikal across the square and called to him. "Hey Mikal! Let's go look at the horses."

They walked together to the paddock where young horses had been brought to sell. "Which one do you like?" Mikal asked, pushing his untidy brown hair back with one hand.

"I like the golden one," said Stefan. "But it doesn't matter. I won't be able to buy a horse for a long time."

"Oh, you'll be running the family farm before very long," Mikal said.

"I wasn't born to be a farmer," Stefan told him. "I'm going over the Dark Mountains in search of adventures. I want to see what lies beyond my pastures."

"You're funny," Mikal laughed, slapping his leg. "No one from the village has ever climbed over the Dark Mountains!"

"Then I shall be the first!" Stefan declared. "I've always felt out of place here, as if I were different somehow from everyone else. I've always wanted more."

That night Stefan dreamed. He dreamed of walking under the towering pine trees, of branches whooshing in the wind over his head. When he woke up, he knew his journey would begin that very day.

Stefan made his announcement at the breakfast table. His parents were quite upset.

"Why must you go so far away?" his mother cried, twisting her apron in her hands. "No one has ever crossed the mountains, and no one has ever come over them into our valley. There must be a reason."

"I can't explain it," Stefan said. "I feel in my heart this is what I am meant to do."

Stefan's father stroked his gray beard thoughtfully. He knew his son had never been completely happy. "Mother, it's time we let Stefan go, to seek out his own way in the world."

All his little brothers and sisters stared in amazement.

Stefan declared, " I'm ready for this quest! I've always longed to explore faraway kingdoms and other lands!"

His brothers admired Stefan's courage. His mother placed bread and meat in a pack, with a gourd container of water. His father embraced him heartily and walked with him to the beginning of the path, giving him advice all the while.

With one last look at the farm where he'd grown up, Stefan slung his pack on his shoulder and began to walk. Already the feeling of adventure sang through his soul.

Chapter II

Sunbeams shone through the early morning mist as Stefan strode up the rough trail that led to the Dark Mountains. After no more than an hour's journey into the thick trees, the trail disappeared completely. His footsteps made no sound on the carpet of fallen pine needles that lay thick underfoot. Sometimes he heard a crackling in the trees or the call of a bird, but he felt very alone. When he became bored, Stefan scooped up a handful of pebbles and tossed them at birds and rabbits to pass the time. After hiking for hours, Stefan sat on a tree stump to rest and eat his lunch from the supplies his mother had packed. Stefan knew he would have to be brave and find his way. The thought of what wonders and magnificent sights lay on the other side of the mountains helped him keep going.

As night fell, Stefan felt doubtful for the first time.

"Great heroes are never afraid," he told himself sternly. His voice sounded small. "I'll build a fire," he said. He set his pack off to the side by a huge tree trunk, then gathered up some old dry sticks and threw them into a pile in the middle of a clearing. The stack was very small, so he pulled some dead-looking branches off nearby trees as well. Odd noises filled the darkness. Just then he heard a rustling noise and quickly jumped around. Two gray squirrels were busily working at the opening of his pack.

Stefan angrily picked up a few stones and threw them toward the animals

to scare them away. Though he only meant to frighten them, one squirrel

ran away on three paws, holding up the front one that had been hit by a

stone. Stefan felt terrible.

"Well, it was my food," he thought. "It's all I have." He took out his

tinderbox and stuck a spark to light the wood.

The fire had blazed high with flames when Stefan leapt to his feet, biting

back a cry of alarm. A huge figure in a dark cloak suddenly appeared at the

edge of the clearing.

"Who dares to use my trees for firewood?" demanded the giant. He strode to Stefan as he spoke, towering over the frightened boy. "Who throws stones at my animals?"

"I…I did, sir," Stefan stammered. "I didn't mean to hurt anything."

"You tore wood off living trees and attacked the children of the forest!" The huge figure roared. "I am the Wizard of the Dark Mountains and these trees and creatures are in my care."

Stefan trembled under the Wizard's fierce gaze. He hadn't made it far without running into trouble!

The Wizard carried a stout wooden staff. His hood shadowed his face and only his blazing eyes could be seen. A red fox padded softly by his side, and birds perched on his large shoulders.

"It's not my fault," said Stefan, his voice shaking. "I had to save my food, didn't I? I had to keep warm."

"That's no excuse!" The Wizard snapped. " You threw stones at animals that weren't after your food, earlier on the trail."

Stefan kept his gaze on the Wizard's, though inside he felt slightly sick. In his heart, he knew what he had done was wrong. Yet what he said was, "I didn't know trees could be hurt, honestly."

"Of course trees can be hurt! I suppose you think animals have no real feelings, either." The Wizard jabbed his staff angrily into the ground.

Without thinking, Stefan said, "Animals can't feel!"
"Ah, but you're wrong!" exclaimed the Wizard, his voice sad. "People like you are the reason I keep the trees and animals safe in the mountains. They have no respect for living things. If you could learn to care for the creatures as I do, then I would not have to frighten you away."

"What do you want me to do?" Stefan wondered.

"There is nothing you can do now," the Wizard said, "Except learn the lesson I send to you."

The boy felt a shiver down his spine. Anything could happen now and he could do nothing to stop it.

The Wizard threw back his hood. A tiny field mouse crept onto his shoulder and the red fox pressed against his legs. Stefan could see that his face looked lined with care. He appeared stern, yet wise, and Stefan's fear lessened.

"Here is my decision." The Wizard announced. "You are to become a bear so that you will know about the lives and feelings of animals."

No sooner had he spoken than Stefan felt a warm tingle all over his body. His world filled with bright light. Next, he was standing on all fours looking down at large furry white paws with enormous claws.

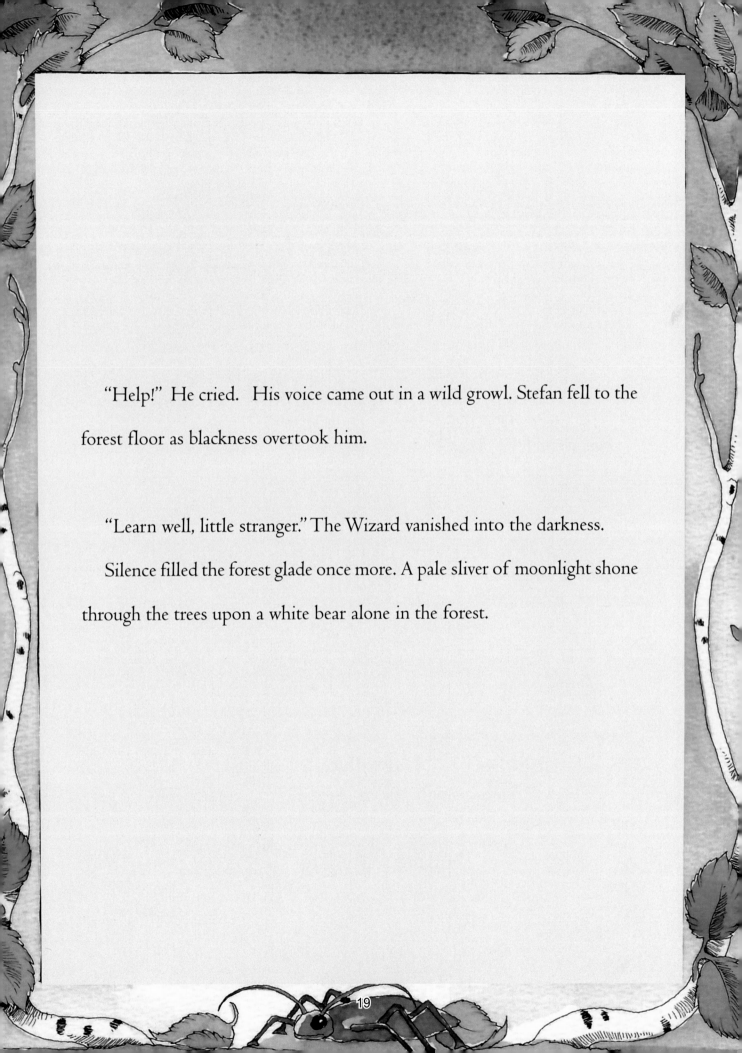

"Help!" He cried. His voice came out in a wild growl. Stefan fell to the forest floor as blackness overtook him.

"Learn well, little stranger." The Wizard vanished into the darkness.

Silence filled the forest glade once more. A pale sliver of moonlight shone through the trees upon a white bear alone in the forest.

Chapter III

A ray of sunlight fell on Stefan's face, awakening him.

"What a strange and awful dream I had!" Stefan thought.

He opened his eyes and saw the charred remains of his fire in the glade's center. Doubt filled his mind. He stretched his cramped limbs and two huge white furry paws appeared in front of him. He sprang to his feet, but he no longer had feet! He looked down at his body and saw exactly what he had feared. He hadn't dreamed the events of last night. He had become a bear!

He looked wildly around the forest glade for the Wizard, racing across the clearing in alarm. Angrily he shook his heavy head.

"I hardly did anything wrong!" he hollered at the trees. "I didn't deserve a punishment this harsh!"

Then, accepting his fate, his large hairy head dipped sorrowfully toward the earth for a long moment.

"What should I do now?" wondered Stefan.

"I'll continue on my journey," he decided aloud with a bearish snarl. "I can't go home now." He crossed the glade, stumbling a bit on his new paws. Soon he was pleased to find how much faster he could move at a bear trot than on his old two legs.

As Stefan went swiftly through the forest, he smelled many new scents with his bear nose. He stopped a moment, closed his eyes and sniffed the air. The aroma of pine came to him, and sweet flowers, and musky earth. There was also a cool sort of smell. His bear senses knew it was water!

Stefan felt very thirsty. He followed his nose to a cool bubbling stream. The water winked with tiny lights in the sunshine, dancing over smooth stones.

As the large white bear pushed through the willows beside the stream, three deer jumped away from the water in fright.

"Wait!" Stefan growled. "I want to talk to you!"

But the deer had run quickly into the forest. Stefan sighed. He bent his head to the water and drank. He could see his wavy reflection in the moving stream.

"I'm very big. I'm scary-looking!" Stefan realized. "No wonder the deer were afraid!"

After he had drunk, he suddenly felt hungry. His sharp bear's eyes saw fish in the stream. Stefan waded in and easily caught some trout with his huge paws. The fresh fish tasted wonderful.

After his meal, he loped rapidly through the woods, traveling many miles. He passed birds and squirrels and foxes, but no beast talked to him. They all ran away before he could show them he was a friendly bear. Stefan began to feel lonely. How could he make friends with the other animals if they wouldn't give him a chance?

A cave Stefan found made a nice bedroom for him that night. His paws were sore from the rough ground and it felt good to lie on the soft earth. He slept deeply, even though the moon shone brightly outside.

Many days passed. Stefan enjoyed being a bear in some ways, but he felt unhappy about the way he looked. He had never felt so alone in all his life. If he hadn't had the wild beauty of the green forest all around him, he would have despaired. He had finally discovered that the earth and trees, the wind and sky had a magic all their own.

"I may not know about the feelings of all animals," thought Stefan, "But I know that bears can be sad and tired."

One day the bear noticed that his way through the forest began to slope steeply downhill. Perhaps he had crossed the Dark Mountains at last! Stefan felt instantly more cheerful.

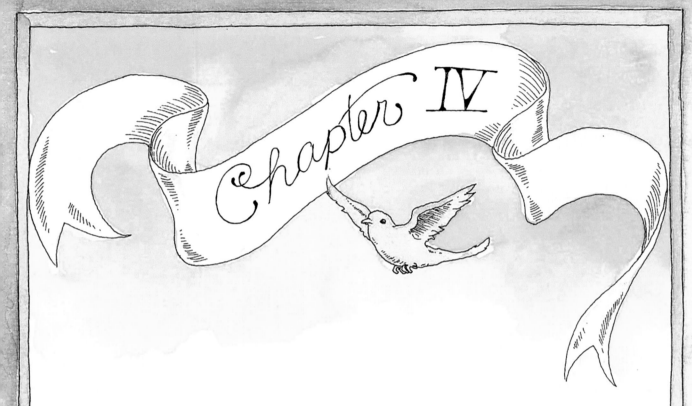

Chapter IV

After traveling for several hours, Stefan's keen bear ears heard human voices and the familiar sounds of a busy town. He climbed out on a ledge where he could see. Below him in the middle of a great expanse of fields many cottages dotted a clearing. A stone fountain cascaded in the center of the village.

He felt suddenly, terribly homesick for his old life and for the company of people like his family. He galloped quickly down out of the dark forest. Eagerly he ran down into the main street of the village, forgetting for the moment that he was no longer Stefan the boy.

Panic spread among the villagers. Women grabbed their children and ran screaming into their homes. Men grabbed poles and poked them at the bear as they backed away.

Stefan stopped in the center of the village. He let out a roar of anguish. They would not talk to him! The people were afraid too, like the small animals!

He howled one last time. The villagers shook with fright. Stefan heard one man say, " I never saw such a big bear, much less a white one! This must have something to do with magic!"

One brave villager came forward towards Stefan. He wore rough homespun clothes, and a battered hat.

"If you are a magic bear, then you can talk. What do you want?" the man demanded.

"I only want to be friends!" Stefan growled gruffly. He was pleasantly surprised that he could speak a little.

"How can we believe you?" the man asked. "You could kill and eat us!"

Stefan protested, "No! I mean you no harm! I was lonely, and I saw your village."

The country people looked at him with fear and anger. Slowly they formed a group, ready to drive him out of the village.

"You don't belong here!" the villager with the hat cried. "Go back to the forest!"

With that, the villagers ran towards him with heavy sticks and clubs. Stefan could have fought them. Instead, he turned and ran back into the trees. He climbed until he was on top of the ledge overlooking the valley again.

Most villagers had gone about their daily chores once more. The bear thought they must have felt very afraid, but wanted to protect their homes and families. Stefan knew then how the squirrels in the forest felt when he threw stones at them to drive them away. He knew how the birds and rabbits felt when he carelessly cast stones at them, not caring if they were hurt. The Dark Wizard was right about people. Now he deeply regretted his thoughtless actions in the woods.

Stefan gazed across the fields. He noticed that the bushy hills west of the village were stirring with activity. Something was happening. He looked closely with his keen eyes.

He could see what looked like a small company of warriors marching toward the town!

"I should let them be attacked after the way they treated me," said Stefan to himself. But then he imagined that it was his old village and his family in danger, and he knew he had to do something to help.

"I hope they will listen to me this time!" Stefan growled. He galloped back down the hill as fast as he could go.

"I've come to warn you!" he roared as he reached the square. "Your village is under attack!"

He hardly noticed the screaming women and children this time. The brave villager once more stood before him.

"Why should we believe you?" the man demanded. "I think it's a trick!"

"Go up in the church tower and look to the West. You can see for yourself! Hurry!"

The man ran to the tower and climbed the steep stairs to the top. He saw that a force of warriors had indeed halted near the village. The soldiers had put down their packs and were readying themselves for battle. Quickly the man rang the church bell as loudly as he could to sound the alarm.

Everyone grabbed whatever weapons they had and prepared to fight. They paid no attention to Stefan. At that moment, he had a good idea. If the villagers were afraid of him, then that army should be, too. Maybe he could scare them away.

He didn't want to think about his plan long enough to be frightened, so he swiftly crossed the fields, then ran on silent paws toward the thick bushes where the enemy hid. Stefan roared in his loud bear's voice as he went charging through the brush.

The warriors turned pale with fear. They meant to attack a helpless village of peasants. They were not ready to fight an enormous mean bear!

The huge animal's snarling mouth was filled with sharp, gleaming teeth. As he ran toward them they could see long, curved claws on his paws. He seemed to be everywhere at once. All the soldiers flung down their weapons and fled for their lives!

Stefan stood on his hind legs and clapped his paws together. His plan had succeeded! He had defeated the entire army! Innocent people would not have to fight and no one would now be hurt. The bear then turned, and loped again to the village square where the townspeople waited.

" My name is Tom," the leader said, smiling this time in welcome. "I'm the Village Mayor. We thank you for saving us from invasion!"

"Who were those men?" Stefan panted.

"They came from a neighboring land. Their ruler is a cruel man who has always wanted to add our country to his own. We have no leader since our king died, leaving us open to their attack," Tom explained. "Now you have defeated our enemies. I think we should make you our king, the King of Cristalla."

Stefan protested, "I have no idea how to be a king."

"Please do it," begged Tom. " Without a ruler, we are always in danger of being taken over by another country. We need you. You can live in the castle on the hill."

Stefan thought about the offer. They hadn't chased him away again. They needed him. Maybe helping the villagers would atone for his mistakes in the Dark Mountains. Besides, if he were king, he could make friends with the people. The women and children stood around him now, colorful in their peasant clothes of red and blue.

"All right," growled the bear, his white fur bright in the sun. "I will be your king and I will always try to protect you." He lifted his head and sniffed the breeze.

The people smiled, clasping hands and hugging each other in relief. They had been saved from the enemy soldiers, and surely no one else would try to defeat the huge bear in battle.

"Follow me," Tom said. "I will show you your new home."

Stefan the bear and Tom, with all the villagers trailing behind, climbed the long winding street up the hill. As they came around a bend, Stefan stopped in wonder. They couldn't mean for him to live here!

Tall windows shone in the sunlight and towers of gray stone reached to the blue sky. Even the large bear felt small as the group passed through huge iron gates and climbed the wide marble steps. Stefan wondered what he had gotten himself into this time!

"What do you expect from your king?" growled Stefan to Tom. He wanted to do a good job and he was only a farm boy himself.

"Every Thursday the people can come to you with problems or disputes. If someone breaks the law, you decide on a punishment. And you are the perfect king to keep us at peace with other countries. The other rulers will be afraid of you!"

Stefan thought, "Afraid of me… like everyone else." And he sighed.

Chapter V

Cristalla was a beautiful land, Stefan thought as he gazed out the castle windows. He could see green farmland spread out below him with clusters of cottages in between. In the distance lay the mysterious deep green of the forest. This land looked much like the home he had left behind. Stefan let out a low whine. He had come all this way to find that life on the far side of the Dark Mountains was little different from life back home. Becoming a bear and being crowned King was certainly an adventure, but he missed his family and friends.

After half the year had passed, Stefan became used to his duties as Cristalla's King and had grown accustomed to his life as an enchanted creature. Some of the villagers shyly spoke to him and the castle workers stopped flinching when he passed. Still, he was growing tired of being a bear. The Wizard's lesson seemed to be taking a long time.

After a few weeks, the castle servants and courtiers noticed that their king seemed sad and silent. They began to talk in small groups, wondering what to do about it. Stefan was large, it was true, but he had been kind to them since he arrived.

The villagers called a town meeting in the old wood and hewn stone church. They wanted to keep their king happy and the kingdom safe.

Tom called the meeting to order. "Who has any ideas?"

A hand went up. An older woman in a gray dress stood. "I think he is lonely," she said.

The crowd murmured. Tom said, "I think Mavis is right. He needs a companion, a wife."

A farmer stood up next. "Where will we find one? We've never seen another bear like him!"

"Maybe one of the village girls would become his wife," Tom said. " She could then be queen."

Everyone agreed to put up notices asking maidens to go to the castle. Perhaps one of them would be willing to marry the king.

Stefan frowned when he heard this plan, but agreed to wait and see. Life in the large castle grew lonelier every day.

Hundreds of girls flocked to the castle on the hill. Some were pretty and some were plain. Some of them ran away screaming, and some of them tried to talk to the bear king even though their knees were shaking. All the maidens agreed they could never marry such a fearsome creature. This made Stefan sadder than ever.

One day, when everyone had given up on the plan, a farmer came to the castle with his daughter.

"My daughter wants to meet the king," he said. "Our farm is poor and my family is hungry. If she were queen, she could help."

Stefan sat upon his throne. "What is your name?" he asked the girl. "I will talk to you only if you are truly willing to do this."

The girl, guided by her father, came closer. Her dark hair fell in lovely waves down her back and her blue dress was crisp and clean. As she turned to Stefan, he could tell her brown eyes were sightless. The girl was blind.

"My name is Lara and I would do anything to help my family," she said in a lovely voice. "That isn't the only reason I wanted to talk to you, though. I know what it is to be different than other people. I thought you might need a friend."

Stefan said, "You must know that I am a great bear. If you could see me, you would be afraid."

Lara came closer, close enough to touch him. Quietly she said, "But your voice is so kind, and your fur is so soft."

Stefan felt a ray of hope. Perhaps this girl would really be a companion for him.

"You shall stay here in the castle as my guest," Stefan decided. "I will have the steward show you and your father to your rooms."

The next five days were wonderful. Lara walked with Stefan in the gardens every day, her hand resting on one large shoulder for guidance. They ate together in the long dining room and walked at night on the castle battlements. Together they talked of many things. Stefan told Lara of how he had always felt different from others even before becoming a bear, and of how he regretted throwing stones at animals. Lara spoke to him of her blindness so bravely that Stefan was ashamed of feeling sorry for himself.

Slowly, they became dear friends. Finally their hearts yearned for each other. At the end of the week Stefan called everybody onto the Great Hall. Richly colored tapestries glowed against the stone walls. Stefan sat on his enormous golden throne.

"I will take Lara as my Queen," Stefan announced. "She will rule you with kindness and love. I promise that her family and all of you will never want for anything."

Lara came fearlessly to the great bear's head and stroked his soft fur. She kissed his dark nose as the villagers cheered with delight.

At that moment, a huge gust of wind blew through the Great Hall. The Wizard of the Dark Mountains appeared in the marble entrance, his cloak flying around him.

"I see you have learned your lesson well, my son," the Wizard pronounced. "You have passed through pain and loneliness and learned to be kind and caring of other creatures. In doing so, you have received a gift that is beyond my power to bestow; that of being loved for yourself."

The great hall was utterly silent as the Wizard raised his staff. "I will take away your bear's form," his deep voice boomed. "Since you have truly changed in your heart, I grant you this boon. You will always have the power to become a bear whenever you wish and I allow you the freedom of the Dark Mountains."

With another blast of air, the Wizard vanished.

And so Stefan ruled many years over the kingdom of Cristalla with Lara as his fair Queen and he always rode a golden steed. He was a wise and patient King, and Lara was ever merry and loving.

Yet now and then he longed to be wild and free again, and he became a huge white bear. With Lara on his back, holding tightly to his fur, he ran swiftly through the forest on silent paws. He told Lara of the rugged beauty around them so she felt she could almost see it. Sometimes they traveled all the way over the Dark Mountains to visit Stefan's family, his old friend Mikal and the rest of the village. Everyone marveled at Stefan's good fortune. And for the rest of his life, he never harmed another living creature.

THE END